First published in 2012 by Hodder Children's Books

Text copyright © Gillian Shields 2012
Illustration copyright © Cally Johnson- Isaacs 2012

Hodder Children's Books, 338 Euston Road, London, NW1 3BH
Hodder Children's Books Australia, Level 17/207 Kent Street,
Sydney, NSW 2000

The right of Gillian Shields to be identified as the author
and Cally Johnson-Isaacs to be identified as the illustrator
of this Work has been asserted by them in accordance
with the Copyright, Designs and Patents Act 1988.

A catalogue record of this book is available from the British Library.

ISBN: 978 1 444 90400 0

Printed in China

Hodder Children's Books is a division
of Hachette Children's Books,
an Hachette UK Company

www.hachette.co.uk

For my darling daughter, my lovely Sasha G.S.
For Dad with love C.J.

Elephantantrum!

Gillian Shields and Cally Johnson-Isaacs

Hodder Children's Books

A division of Hachette Children's Books

Ellie had **everything**.

But she wanted more. She wanted an elephant.

She wouldn't eat or sleep or brush her hair.
She wouldn't smile or play or do her lessons.
She wouldn't even get out of bed
until she got what she wanted.

'Please get up, Ellie,' said her father.

'NO!' she replied. 'Not until you get me an ELEPHANT!'

Ellie's father went to his big fancy office.

He wrote letters and made phone calls.

He worked and worried and fussed and fretted until...

THIS WAY UP!

...an elephant arrived for Ellie.

Ellie jumped up and down in excitement. She couldn't wait to boss her new elephant around.

'Come here, Elephant!' she said.
'Give me a ride! Do a trick!
Pick up my toys!'

The elephant wrapped his trunk around Ellie's waist and lifted her up.

'Ooh!' said Ellie.

'Put me down!'

But the elephant took a good long look at her...

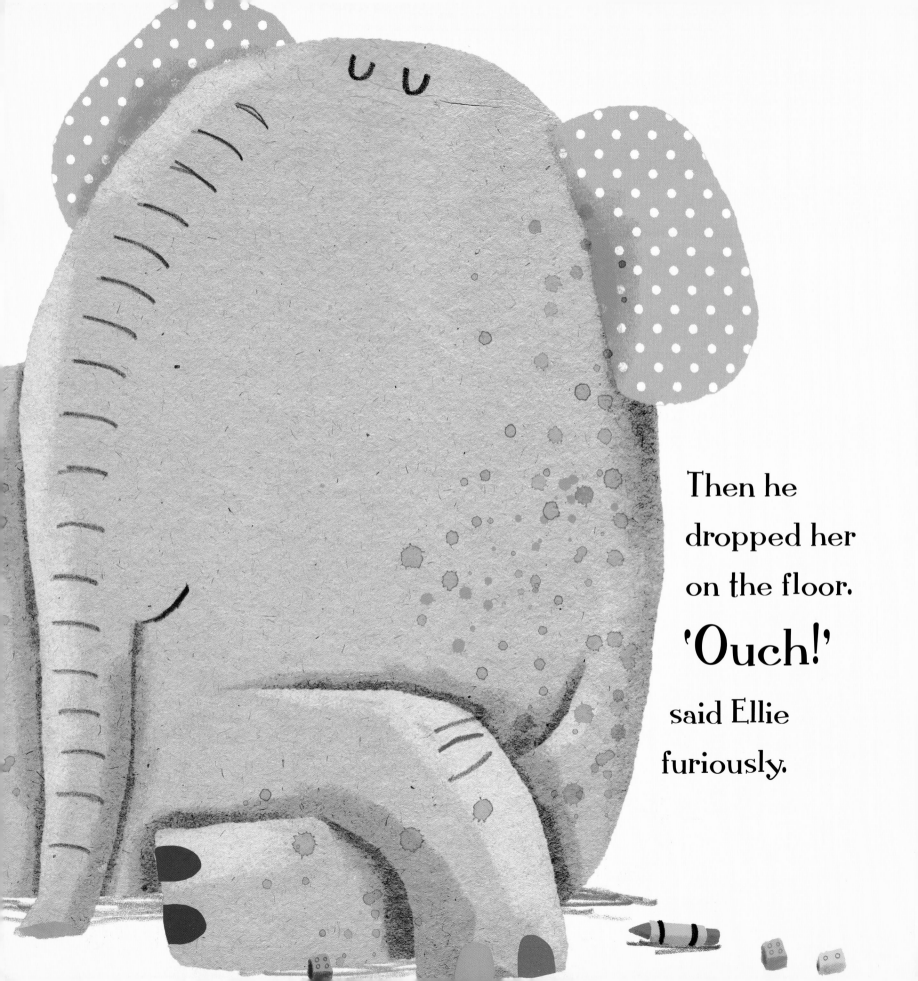

Then he dropped her on the floor. 'Ouch!' said Ellie furiously.

She had a terrible tantrum.

'I don't want **that** elephant,' she shouted.

'Get me a different one!'

'But it's an extraordinary elephant,' said her father wisely.
'I think it's just the one you need.'

So the elephant stayed and made himself at home.
He slept in Ellie's bed.

He wore her best clothes.

He ate her breakfast.

He played with her toys.

'But they're mine!' Ellie howled.

The elephant took no notice. He even went to school and sat in Ellie's place and played with Ellie's friends.

'Go away!' Ellie ordered.

But the elephant ignored her.

Now the elephant had everything. Ellie even had to make his sandwiches and clean his boots and fold his handkerchiefs. He didn't say 'please' or 'thank you'.

And if Ellie didn't do exactly what he wanted...

eleph

...he had an
enormous

ntantrum!

Ellie started to cry. The elephant passed
her a handkerchief.

'Thank you,' said Ellie.
It was the first time she had
ever said 'thank you'.

Then Ellie said,
'Please can I have my
things back?'

'Why don't we share them?'
said the elephant.

'All right,' said Ellie happily.
'Let's share.'

So they played together
and it was **brilliant**.

When they went to school, Ellie said,

'Would you **please** give my friends a ride

in the playground?'

'Of course,' said the elephant.

'**Thank you,**' said Ellie.

They all took turns, EVEN Ellie.

It was fun.

It was extraordinary!

That night, Ellie said, 'I hope you'll stay forever.'

'I can't,' said the elephant gently. 'There are other children who need me too. You'll have to share me.'

Ellie didn't scream or shout or have a tantrum. 'I understand,' she said.

And when she woke up, the elephant had gone…

To Ellie
See you soon   x

...almost.